Pooh

Piglet

Pooh

eOR

Rabbits

E. P. Dutton   New York

POOH's
Counting Book

❀ by A. A. MILNE ❀

illustrations by E. H. Shepard

Compilation copyright © 1982 by Michael John Brown,
Peter Janson-Smith, Roger Hugh Vaughan Charles Morgan, and
David Macbeth Moir Carey, Trustees of the Pooh Properties

Individual copyrights for text and illustrations:
Winnie-the-Pooh, Copyright, 1926, by E. P. Dutton & Co.,
Inc. Copyright Renewal, 1954, by A. A. Milne. *Now We
Are Six*, Copyright, 1927, by E. P. Dutton & Co., Inc.
Copyright Renewal, 1955, by A. A. Milne. *The House at
Pooh Corner*, Copyright, 1928, by E. P. Dutton & Co.,
Inc. Copyright Renewal, 1956, by A. A. Milne.

Library of Congress Cataloging in Publication Data
Milne, A. A. (Alan Alexander), 1882–1956.
Pooh's counting book.
Summary: The numbers one to ten are introduced
by appropriate excerpts from the author's poems and
prose about Christopher Robin and his friends.
1. Counting—Juvenile literature.   [1. Counting]
I. Shepard, Ernest H. (Ernest Howard), 1879–1976, ill.
II. Title.
QA113.M54 1982   513'.2   82-5170
ISBN 0-525-44016-X   AACR2

Published in the United States by E. P. Dutton, Inc.,
2 Park Avenue, New York, N.Y. 10016

Published simultaneously in Canada by
McClelland and Stewart Ltd.,
25 Hollinger Road, Toronto, Ontario M4B 3G2

Quotations selected by
and book designed by Riki Levinson

Printed in the U.S.A.
10 9 8 7 6 5 4 3 2

When I was ONE,
I had just begun.

When I was TWO,
I was nearly new.

When I was THREE,
I was hardly me.

When I was FOUR,
I was not much more.

When I was FIVE,
I was just alive.

But now I am SIX, I'm as clever as clever,
So I think I'll be SIX now for ever and ever.

1

"I'm giving this to Eeyore," Pooh explained, "as a present. What are *you* going to give?"

"Couldn't I give it too?" said Piglet. "From both of us?"

"No," said Pooh. "That would *not* be a good plan."

"All right, then, I'll give him a balloon. I've got ONE left from my party. I'll go and get it now, shall I?"

"That, Piglet, is a *very* good idea."

ONE

Wherever I am, there's always Pooh,
There's always Pooh and Me.
Whatever I do, he wants to do,
"Where are you going today?" says Pooh:
"Well, that's very odd 'cos I was too.
Let's go together," says Pooh, says he.
"Let's go together," says Pooh.

So wherever I am, there's always Pooh,
  There's always Pooh and Me.
"What would I do?" I said to Pooh,
  "If it wasn't for you," and Pooh said: "True,
  It isn't much fun for One, but TWO
  Can stick together," says Pooh, says he.
"That's how it is," says Pooh.

TWO

3 Cheers for Pooh!
(*For who?*)
For Pooh—
3 Cheers for Bear!
(*For where?*)
For Bear—
3 Cheers for the wonderful
   Winnie-the-Pooh!
(*Just tell me, somebody—*
   WHAT DID HE DO?)

3

THREE

There were **FOUR** *animals in front of them!*

"Do you see, Piglet? Look at their tracks! Three, as it were, Woozles, and one, as it was, Wizzle. *Another Woozle has joined them!*"

4

FOUR

Berryman and Baxter,
Prettiboy and Penn
And old Farmer Middleton
Are FIVE big men...
And all of them were after
The Little Black Hen.

5

FIVE

They were out of the snow now, but it was very cold, and to keep themselves warm they sang Pooh's song right through SIX times, Piglet doing the tiddely-poms and Pooh doing the rest of it, and both of them thumping on the top of the gate with pieces of stick at the proper places.

6

SIX

"Do you remember when I said that a Respectful Pooh Song might be written about You Know What?"

"Did you, Pooh?" said Piglet, getting a little pink around the nose. "Oh, yes, I believe you did."

"It's been written, Piglet."

"Has it, Pooh?" he asked huskily.

7

"There are SEVEN verses in it."

"SEVEN?" said Piglet, as carelessly as he could. "You don't often get SEVEN verses in a Hum, do you, Pooh?"

SEVEN

EIGHT eights are sixty-four;
   Multiply by seven.
When it's done,
Carry one,
   And take away eleven.

8

EIGHT

"Pooh isn't there," Owl said.

"Not there?"

"Has *been* there. He's been sitting on a branch of his tree outside his house with NINE pots of honey. But he isn't there now."

"Oh, Pooh!" cried Christopher Robin. "Where *are* you?"

"Here I am," said a growly voice behind him.

"Pooh!"

They rushed into each other's arms.

9

NINE

O Timothy Tim
  Has **TEN** pink toes,
  And **TEN** pink toes
Has Timothy Tim.
They go with him
  Wherever he goes,
  And wherever he goes
They go with him.

10

TEN

Katiga

WOL